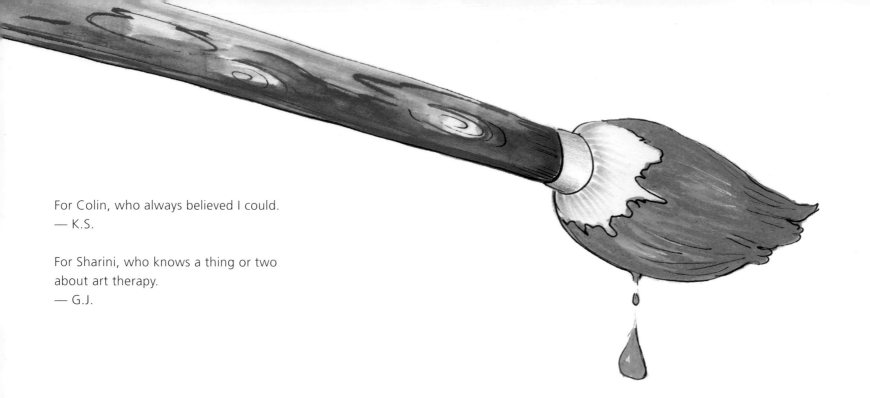

For Colin, who always believed I could.
— K.S.

For Sharini, who knows a thing or two
about art therapy.
— G.J.

First published 2018

EK Books
an imprint of Exisle Publishing Pty Ltd
PO Box 864, Chatswood, NSW 2057, Australia
226 High Street, Dunedin, 9016, New Zealand
www.ekbooks.org

A CiP record for this book is available from the
National Library of Australia.

ISBN 978-1-925335-69-9

Designed by Big Cat Design
Typeset in Minya Nouvelle 18 on 28pt
Printed in China

This book uses paper sourced under ISO 14001 guidelines
from well-managed forests and other controlled sources.

10 9 8 7 6 5 4 3 2 1

Finding Granny

KATE SIMPSON & GWYNNETH JONES

EK

Edie's Granny is a playtime Granny, a bedtime, story-time pantomime Granny, an I'm not afraid of some slime Granny.

Edie's Granny is an ice cream Granny, a winter night snuggle up tight Granny, an everything will be all right Granny.

Best of all, Edie's Granny is a
love as fierce as a lion Granny.

That's simply the Granny she is. Until ...

There's a hospital bed with Granny's name on it,
but the lady inside doesn't look like Granny.
When she tries to speak, the words come out wrong.

'That's not my Granny!'

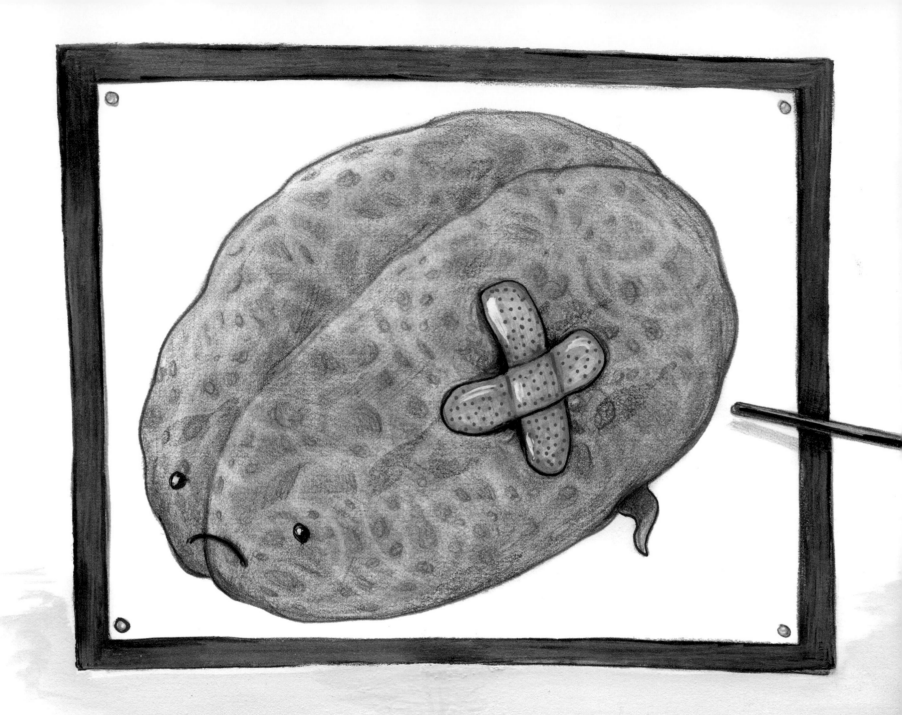

'Your Granny's had a stroke,' says the doctor.
'Her brain isn't working the way it used to.'

Edie shakes her head. Her Granny is a fiery
Granny, an I can do anything you can Granny.
Her Granny doesn't need help eating dinner.

Edie comes to the
hospital every day.

She waits in the corridor.

One day, Granny's
hospital bed is empty.

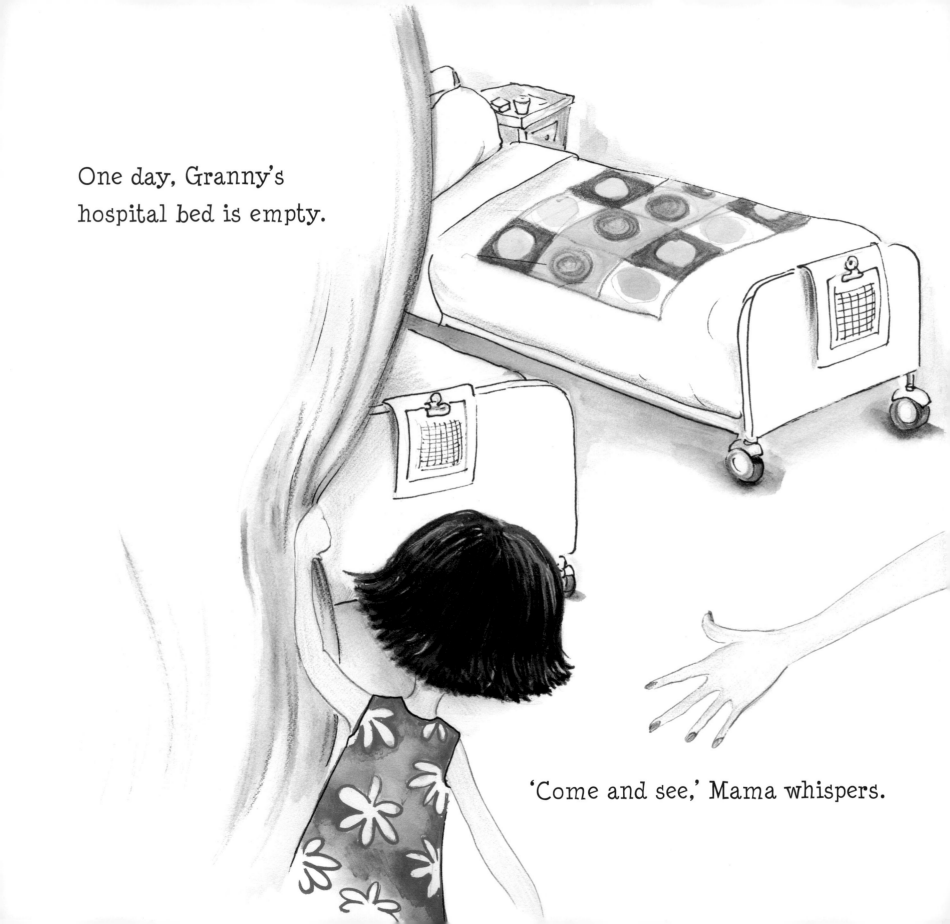

'Come and see,' Mama whispers.

'What's she doing?' asks Edie.

'It's an art class. Painting helps Granny's
brain learn new things and making
something beautiful helps her feel
stronger. At the end of the year, the
hospital will have an exhibition.'

Something beautiful?
Edie thinks. Granny's
vase of flowers looks like
it's about to fall over
and the colours are all
running into each other.

Granny's hand wobbles as she stretches her paintbrush out for more paint: red, then green, then ...

'Hey!' Edie cries.

And then Granny is
laughing, laughing, laughing.

Edie comes to the
hospital every day.

She and Granny are working on a painting for the exhibition. The vase is still a little wobbly and sometimes the colours run into each other, but Mama is right. It *is* beautiful.

'It will be a little while
before she can come
home,' says Mama.

'I know,' says Edie.

'And things might
be different.'

'That's okay,' says Edie.

She looks at Granny. Things *are* different,
but some things haven't changed.

Granny is still a playtime Granny, a bedtime, story-time pantomime Granny, an I'm not afraid of some slime Granny.

Granny is still an ice cream Granny,
a winter night snuggle up tight Granny,
an everything will be all right Granny.

Best of all, Granny is still a love as
fierce as a lion Granny.

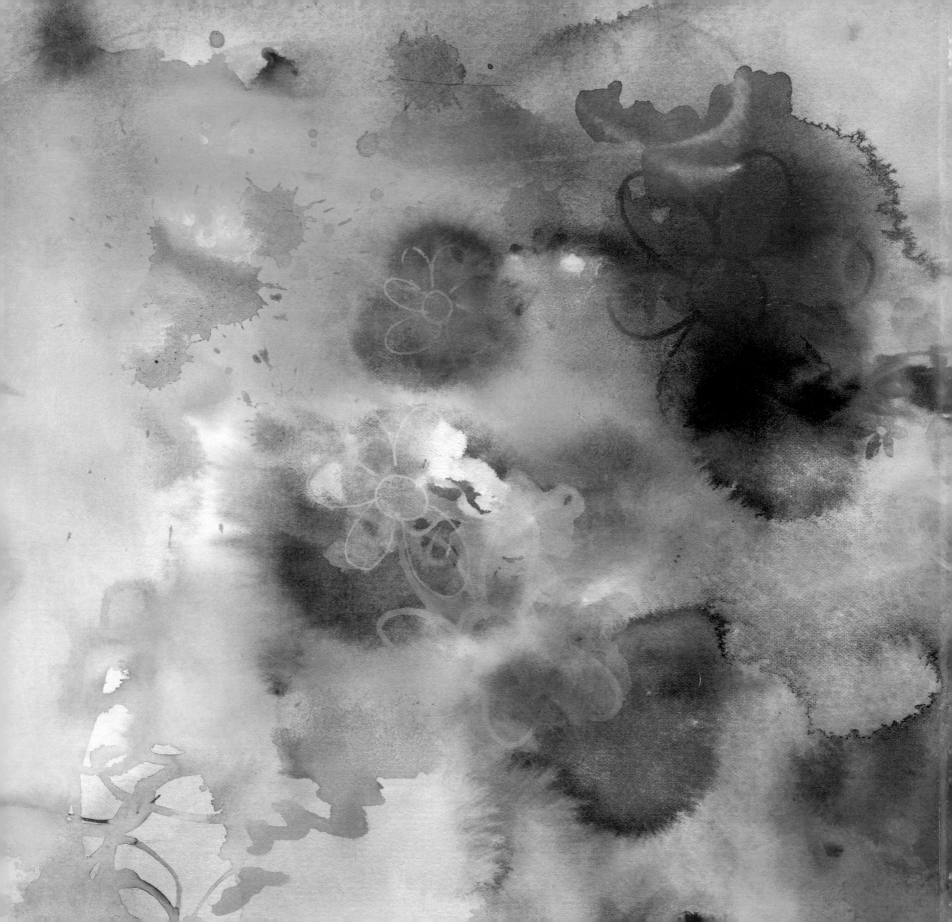